HISTORY QUICK RE/

Stories of Tudor T

By Alan Child

Illustrated by Gillian Marklew

ANGLIA *young* BOOKS

First published in 1995
by Anglia Young Books
an imprint of Mill Publishing
PO Box 120
Bangor
BT19 7BX
Reprinted 2001, 2006

© 1995 Alan Childs

All rights reserved. No part of this publication may be reproduced, stored in a retrieval system, or transmitted in any form or by any means, electronic, mechanical, photocopying, recording or otherwise without the written permission of the Publisher.

Illustrations by Gillian Marklew

British Library Cataloguing-in-Publication Data
A catalogue record for this book is available from the British Library

ISBN 1 871173 44 2

Typeset in Sassoon Primary by Goodfellow & Egan, Cambridge and printed in Great Britain by Ashford Colour Press Ltd., Gosport, Hampshire.

CONTENTS

	Page
THE KING'S SHIP (1545)	1
Glossary	17
Historical Notes	18
THE WOMAN IN BLACK (1585)	21
Glossary	39
Historical Notes	40
MASTER WILL'S NEW THEATRE (1599)	43
Glossary	58
Historical Notes	59

THE KING'S SHIP
1545

Tom Kemp was tired. It was still early in the morning, but he had been walking since dawn. Just outside Portsmouth, he sat down on a grassy bank and watched the crowds pushing through the gateway into the town.

A young man sat down beside him and unwrapped a <u>cloth bundle</u>. He took out a flat loaf of bread and two apples.

He looked at Tom. 'Want some breakfast?' he asked.

Tom nodded gratefully and took some bread.

'My name's Kit Calthorpe,' said the young man. 'I'm a carpenter and I've come to Portsmouth to find work.'

He took a bite of apple. 'What about you?'

Tom felt inside his <u>doublet</u> and pulled out a letter. He showed it to Kit.

'It's from my father,' he said. 'His friend is the captain of a ship and I'm going to be the ship's <u>cabin-boy</u>.'

'What's the name of the ship?' asked Kit, but Tom didn't answer. He was looking at some soldiers riding up to the town gate. They were shouting at the crowds to make way.

'What's happening?' asked Tom.

'It's the King!' said someone. 'King Henry's coming!'

The people ran to each side of the roadway. In the distance, Kit and Tom saw some more soldiers and then, behind the soldiers, a carriage. As the carriage clattered past, the crowd shouted and cheered, and Kit and Tom saw the old King inside.

'Why has the King come to Portsmouth?' asked Tom. Kit shrugged, but a man in the crowd said, 'He's come to see his ships go off to fight the French. They'll sail today if the wind is in the right direction.'

Tom pulled at Kit's arm. 'Did you hear that?' he said, excitedly. 'The ships are sailing today and I'll be sailing too!'

Kit and Tom followed the crowd through the gate and into the narrow streets. Soldiers and sailors were everywhere.

They walked down to the harbour and watched boats taking supplies to the large ships. On one boat they saw cannon-balls, rope and boxes of arrows.

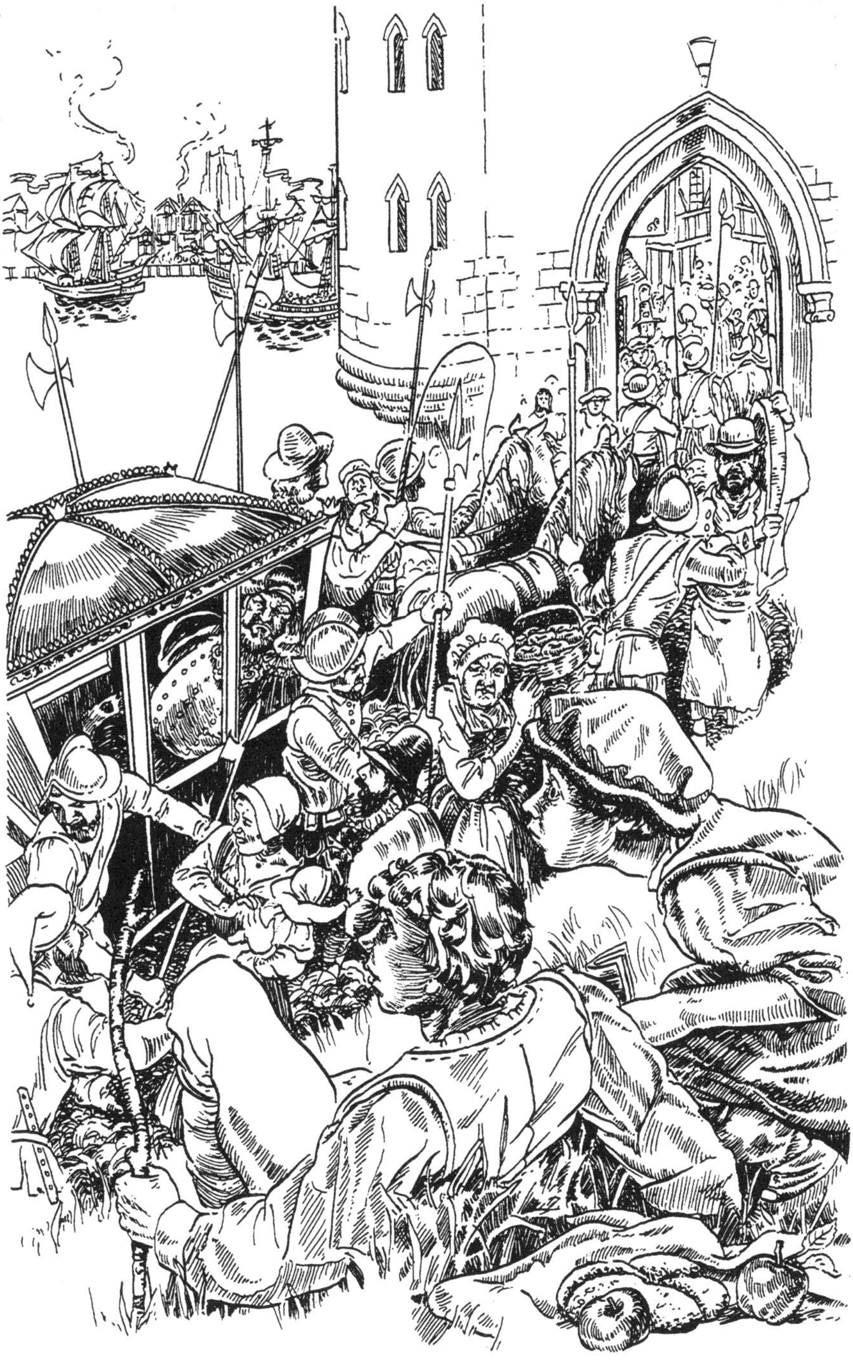

Some barrels were being loaded onto another boat. One of the barrels was split open and they could smell the salted fish inside.

But there was an even better smell coming from a nearby cookhouse. A smell of hot meat pies. Kit sniffed. 'Pity I haven't got any money,' he said.

Tom pulled out his leather purse. 'I've got some money,' he said, taking out a few coins. 'I'll buy two pies for us.'

In his hurry, Tom dropped the coins. One of the coins was made of gold. Kit picked it up and gave it back.

'Where did you get that?' he whispered.

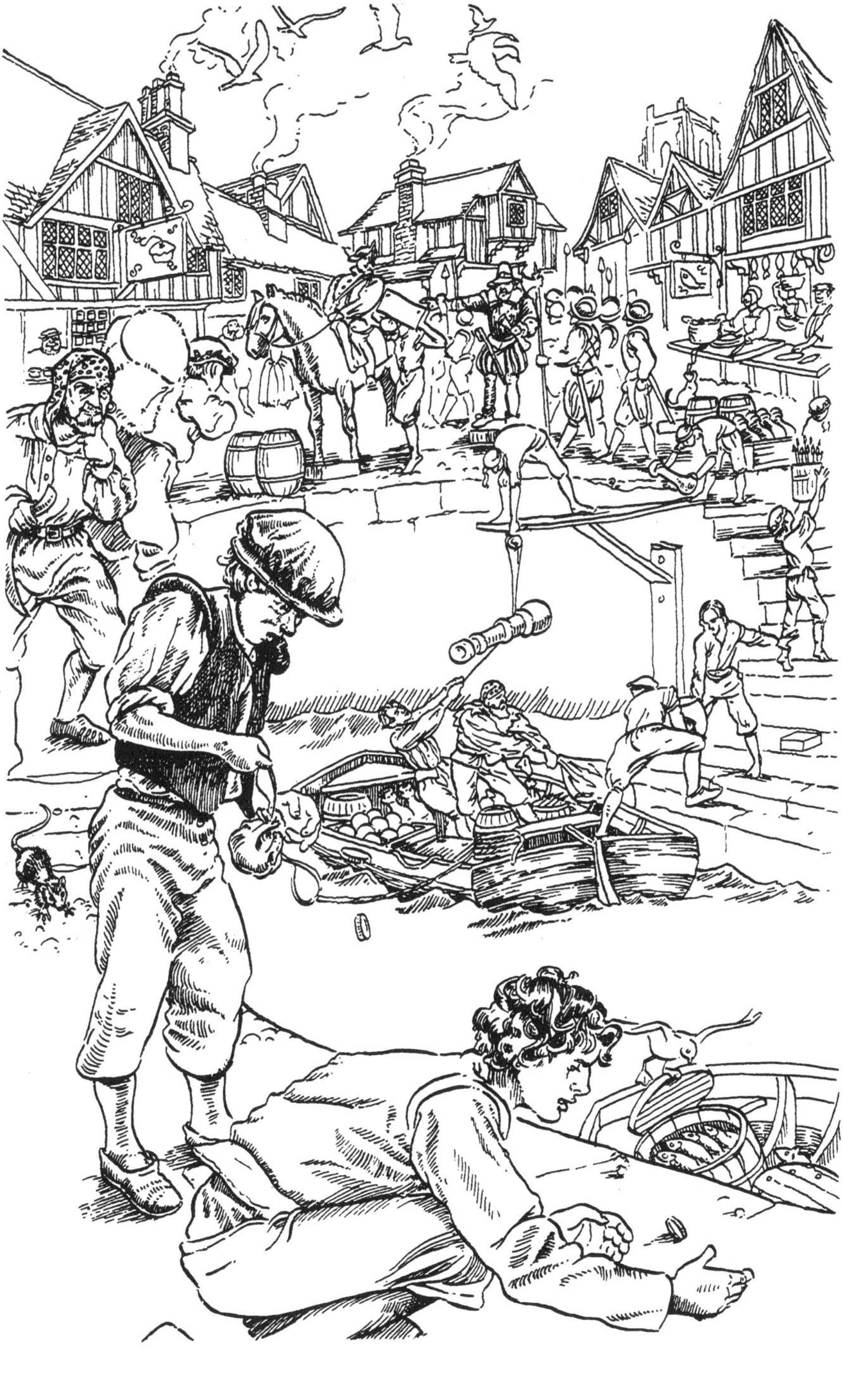

Quickly, Tom put it back in his purse and looked round nervously. 'That's my lucky gold <u>angel</u>,' he said. 'My father gave it to me.'

A rough-looking man had also seen Tom drop the gold coin. He stopped for a moment, then he walked away. Neither Kit nor Tom noticed him.

Tom said to Kit. 'If I buy you a pie, will you help me get to my ship?'

Kit smiled and nodded, then he turned back to look at the sea.

Tom bought the pies, but just as he came out of the cookhouse, he was grabbed from behind. The pies went flying and Tom was dragged into a dark alley.

He tried to scream, but a man's hand covered his mouth. He struggled and kicked, but it was no use. His attacker held him firmly.

Then Tom tripped. He fell hard and knocked his head. Everything went black.

When Tom woke up, Kit was beside him. Tom sat up slowly. His head ached and he felt sick and dizzy. His purse had gone!

'What's happened, Kit?' he mumbled. 'Where's my gold angel?'

'I don't know,' said Kit. 'I think you were attacked by a <u>cutpurse</u>. I've been looking for you for ages.' He helped Tom to his feet and led him out of the alley.

'Quickly,' said Kit. 'We may be too late. The wind has changed and the King's ships are sailing. We must hurry!'

Kit held Tom's arm and they pushed their way through the crowd down to the water's edge.

'Which is your ship?' asked Kit.

Tom pointed. 'That one,' he said. 'The big one with four masts.'

'It's not far away,' said Kit. 'We may still be in time.'

They ran down the stone steps leading to the water. Kit leapt into the nearest rowing boat and Tom followed. A man shouted at them from up on the wall, but they took no notice.

Kit started rowing.

'Quick!' said Tom. They're getting ready to sail. The anchor is coming up!'

Tom watched the sails unfurl and fill with wind.

Kit sweated as he rowed. They were nearly there! They could see the men on the deck and the grey cannons poking out from the gun-doors.

Then, as Tom watched, the great ship began to lean over. It leant further and further until the gun-doors were in the sea! Water began to pour into the ship.

'What's happening Kit?' shouted Tom.

Kit stopped rowing and turned to look. All along the harbour wall, people were staring too. They had been cheering but now they were silent as the great ship leant over, closer and closer to the waves.

Shouts and screams came from the soldiers and sailors on board as they started sliding down the decks. Some leapt into the sea.

Kit and Tom saw a sailor in the water. Quickly, Kit rowed over to him. They grabbed at his clothes and pulled him into the boat.

Now other small boats were coming to help. Kit and Tom rowed for shore,

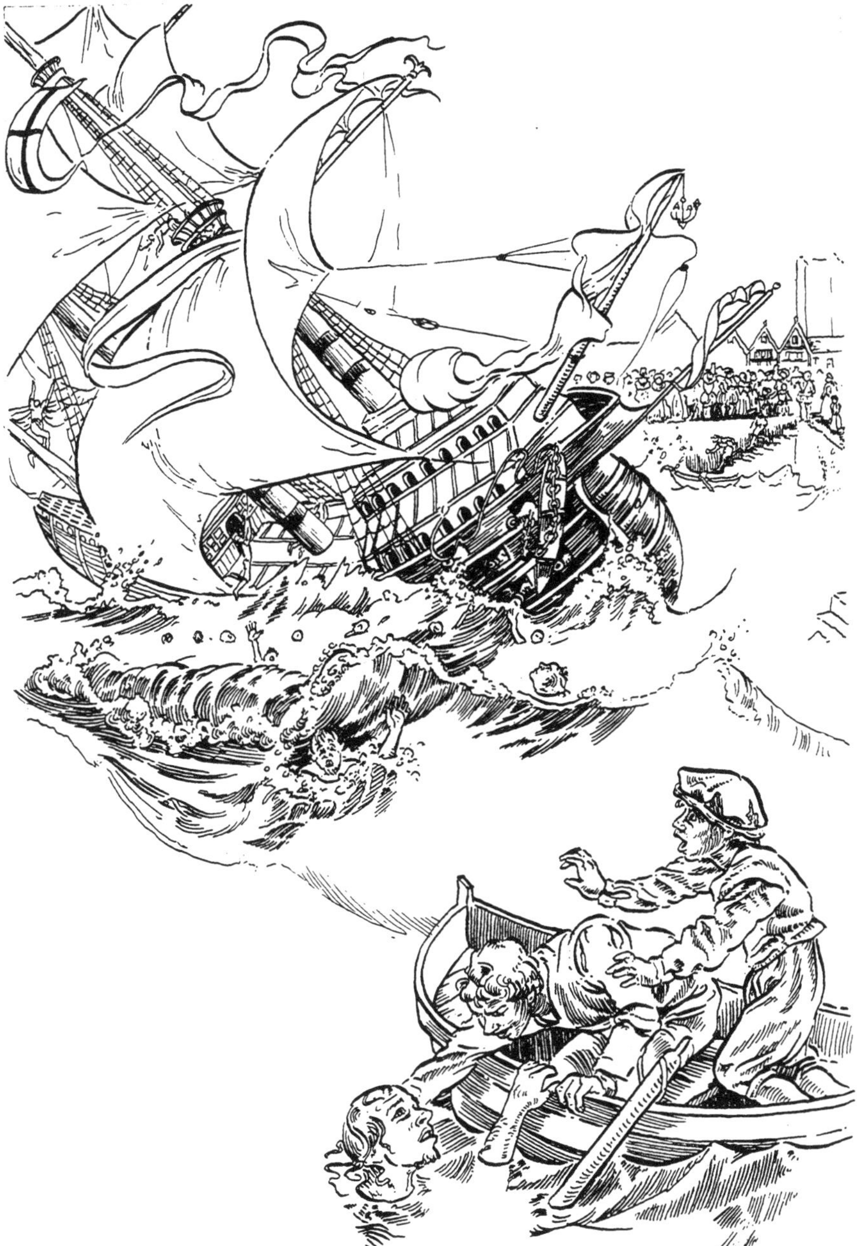

then back again and again to try to rescue drowning sailors. Often they were too late, but they still went on looking until darkness fell.

The next day, they sat on the harbour wall and stared at the water. Tom pulled out his father's letter:

'To Captain Roger Grenville
His Majesty's ship, Mary Rose'

Everyone in Portsmouth was talking about the disaster. There had been 700 men on board the Mary Rose. Now, only 40 of those men were still alive.

If it hadn't been for the cutpurse, Tom would have been on board the Mary Rose.

Tom read his father's letter again and thought of all the dead sailors. He thought of his father's friend, Captain Grenville. And he thought of his own lucky escape – saved by his lucky angel!

'Will you go home now?' asked Kit.

Tom was silent for a moment, then he said, slowly, 'I must get word to my family that I am safe, but I don't want to go home. I still want to be a cabin-boy, so I'll find another ship, if I can.'

He threw a pebble into the water. 'What will you do, Kit?'

Kit grinned. 'Perhaps I'll get a job on the same ship as you. We can look for work together.'

'I'd like that,' said Tom. Then he added, quietly, 'If it hadn't been for you, I might be dead. I'm lucky to be alive.'

'I think you will always be lucky, Tom,' said Kit.

GLOSSARY

<u>angel</u>
a gold coin, called an angel-noble. It showed St Michael and a dragon. It was worth one third of a pound

<u>cabin boy</u>
on ships at this time, and later, young boys were taken on as part of the crew, to do the odd jobs

<u>cloth bundle</u>
a useful way of carrying a few belongings, was to wrap them in a piece of cloth. Sometimes the cloth was tied to a stick

<u>cutpurse</u>
when leather purses were tied to people's belts, a cutpurse was a thief who cut the strings to steal the purse

<u>doublet</u>
a Tudor jacket, often without sleeves

<u>gun-doors</u>
ships had cannons on board, and small hinged doors covered the holes where the guns fired from in battle

HISTORICAL NOTES for THE KING'S SHIP

The Mary Rose was built at Portsmouth in 1509–10, when King Henry VIII was young. It was named after his sister Mary, and was his favourite ship. As a new ship it fought well against the French.

In the summer of 1545 the Mary Rose, under her captain Roger Grenville, was getting ready to fight the French again. It had been rebuilt a few years earlier and must have looked a fine sight that Sunday in July, when the tragedy happened.

No-one really knows why the Mary Rose sank. Some people think it was top-heavy because of all the extra soldiers and guns on board. Perhaps the captain tried to turn too suddenly.

King Henry had come to Portsmouth especially, to watch the English ships leaving the harbour.

In 1982, after many years of searching, the Mary Rose was at last rescued from her grave at the bottom of the sea. It was a great day for everyone who had worked so hard, including Prince Charles, one of Henry VIII's descendants.

Today the Mary Rose can be seen in a special building, where she is being restored. There are also thousands of Tudor objects in a museum nearby. They tell us what life was like for cabin boys like Tom.

THE WOMAN IN BLACK
1585

It was Christmas Eve at <u>Chartley Manor</u> and there was a lot to do. Jane and Gilbert were helping their father, who was an important servant in the house. Their father wanted everything to be perfect for the new Master, <u>Sir Amias</u>.

Jane and Gilbert had helped to bring

the <u>Yule log</u> in from the park to lie across the fire. Now they were helping to decorate the great hall.

But their father was not satisfied. 'We need more holly,' he shouted.

Jane and Gilbert picked up some baskets and went outside. They crossed the frozen <u>moat</u> and ran into the woods. Their fingers grew numb with cold as they tore at the spiky holly.

It was dark by the time they walked back to the house but the candles had been lit and a soft light shone from the windows.

They were passing the main door when Jane suddenly stopped.

'Listen!' she said.

A <u>coach</u> was coming up the drive and it was travelling very fast. It stopped at the door and some men jumped out.

'They're soldiers!' whispered Gilbert. Then someone else got out of the coach. A woman, followed by two dogs.

The main door opened, shedding light on the woman. Jane and Gilbert saw that she was dressed all in black. Then one of the soldiers took the woman's arm and led her quickly into the house.

Jane and Gilbert hurried through the servants' door and went back to the great hall. But the woman in black was nowhere to be seen.

Their father wasn't in the great hall either, so they went to look for him. They found him in the kitchen, cleaning the big silver plates for the Christmas feast.

Jane and Gilbert rushed up to him.

'Father,' said Jane, 'A visitor has just arrived. A woman in black. And she had soldiers with her. Who is she?'

Their father looked up quickly.

'Be quiet!' he hissed. 'Don't speak of this to anyone.'

'But who is she?' asked Gilbert.

'I can't tell you, Gilbert, but I want you both to keep your ears and your

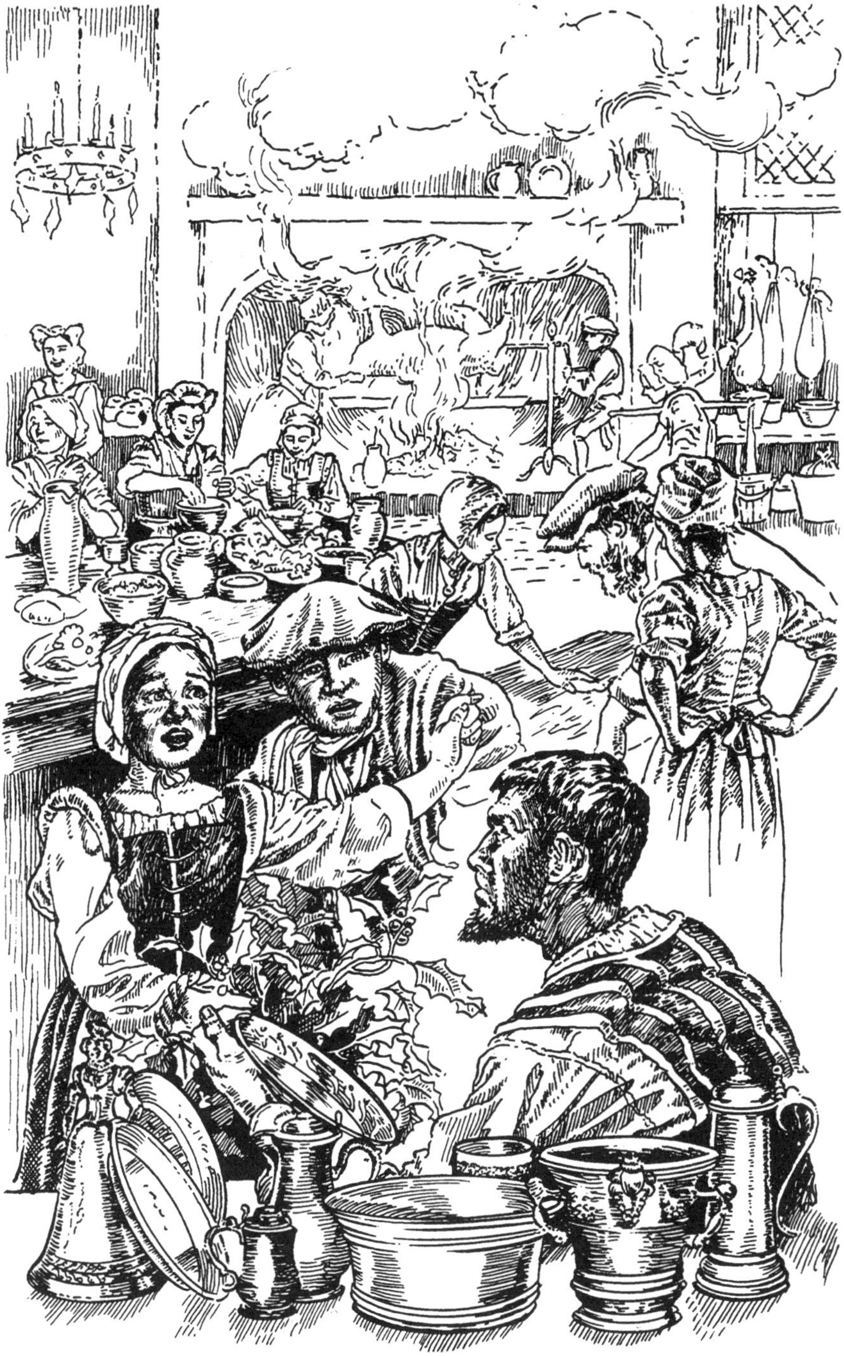

eyes open. Watch and listen! This house may become a house of secrets and you must tell me if you see or hear anything strange.'

'But ...' began Jane.

'Quiet!' said their father sternly. 'No more questions! And remember, don't speak of this to anyone. It is our secret.'

Christmas was so exciting that Gilbert and Jane almost forgot about the woman in black. There was wonderful food for the Christmas feast. Roast swan, meat pasties, purple jellies and <u>tansy</u> pudding.

There were games, too, and singing and dancing, and a play about Saint George and the Dragon.

A few weeks after Christmas, Jane and Gilbert were fetching water from the well. As they filled their jugs, they saw a horse and cart come to the servants' door. The cart was loaded with barrels of beer.

Gilbert walked over and held the horse's head.

Usually, Gilbert helped the driver unload the barrels. But today, there was a different driver and he didn't want any help.

The man seemed nervous. 'Out of my way,' he shouted, 'or you'll find a heavy barrel on your toe.' Then he started to take the barrels inside the house.

Jane and Gilbert took their jugs of water to the kitchen. When they came out to the well again, they stopped in surprise.

The driver of the beer cart had a knife in his hand. He was scratching something on the side of the last barrel left on the cart. Then he took the barrel inside. He didn't notice Jane and Gilbert.

'What was he doing that for?' whispered Gilbert.

Jane frowned. 'I think he was marking the barrel,' she said slowly.

'Marking the barrel?' said Gilbert. 'Why should he do that?'

'I don't know,' said Jane, 'but Father said we must keep our eyes and ears open. Perhaps we should take a look.'

After they had filled the last water jug, Jane and Gilbert crept down the passage to the <u>cellar</u>. No one saw them as they climbed down the dark steps.

At the bottom of the steps, a candle was burning, casting shadows. It was very quiet in the cellar and very damp. The only sound was the sound of dripping water.

Jane and Gilbert found the barrels, but it was too dark to see which one was marked. They were just going to fetch the candle, when the cellar door opened and somone came hurrying down the steps.

'Quick, let's hide!' whispered Gilbert. 'We'll be in terrible trouble if we are caught.'

They crouched down behind the barrels. They hardly dared to breathe.

They saw a man dressed in servants' uniform come into the cellar. He took the candle and walked over to the barrels, peering at each one in turn. Suddenly he gave a grunt. He put the candle down and started pulling at something on one of the barrels.

'I think he's found the barrel with the mark!' whispered Jane.

They watched the man remove the wooden peg which fitted into the hole at the top of the barrel. Then he put his fingers into the hole and drew something out.

'It's a bag!' whispered Gilbert.

The man put the bag inside his shirt and replaced the wooden peg firmly in the hole, then he put the candle back and hurried away up the steps. Jane and Gilbert waited until the cellar door had closed, then they crept up the steps and peered out into the passage.

'There he is!' said Jane. 'He's going upstairs.'

The man was walking fast and Jane and Gilbert had to hurry to keep sight of him. At the top of the stairs, the man slowed down. Jane and Gilbert hid behind a curtain.

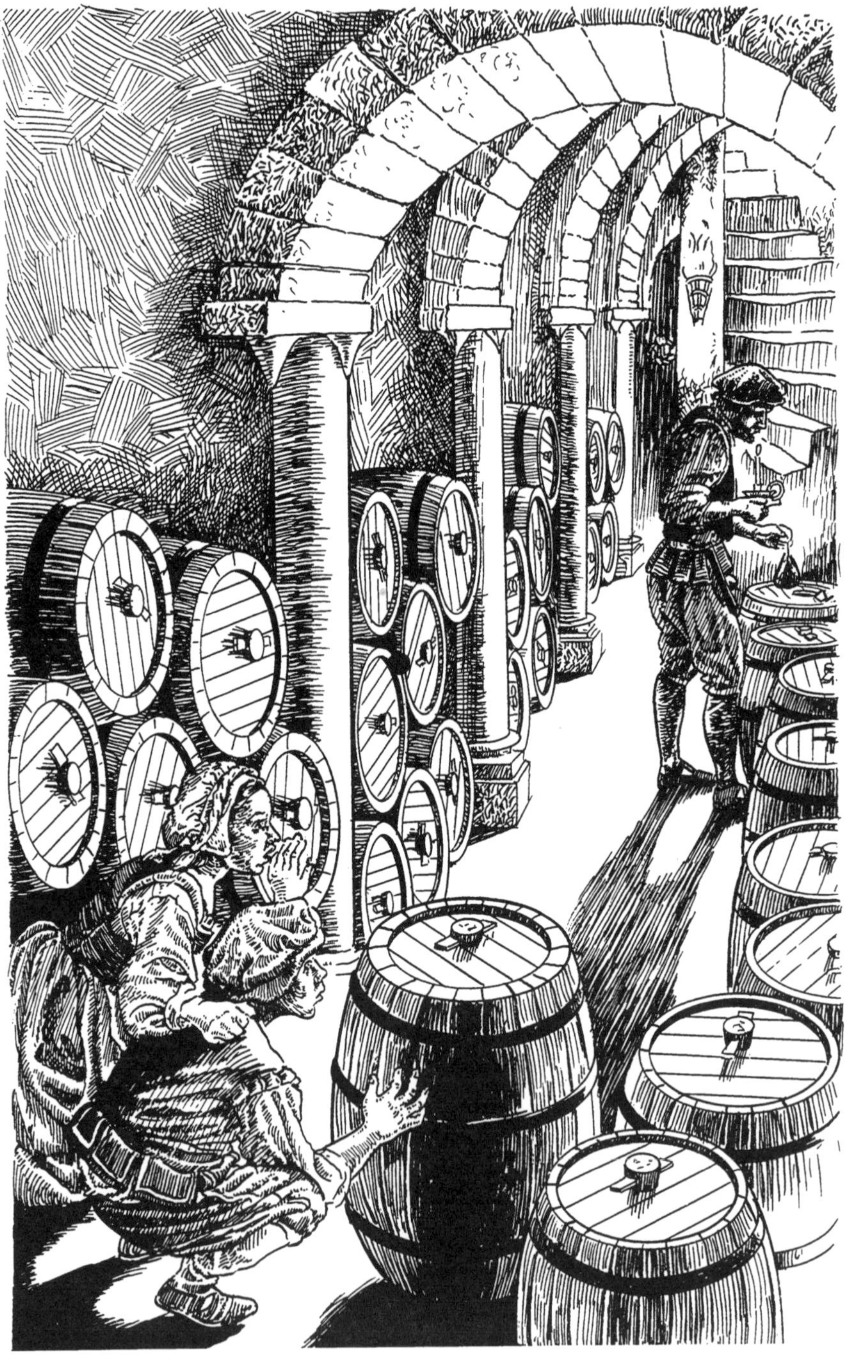

The man looked to left and right, then he took the bag from his shirt and knocked four times, very gently, on one of the bedrooms doors. The door opened for a second and Jane and Gilbert saw a woman's hand take the bag. Then the servant walked quickly away.

But suddenly there was a yapping noise and the bedroom door was pushed open again. A dog bounded out and headed for the stairs.

Jane and Gilbert left their hiding place and ran after it. Gilbert got to it first, snatched it up in his arms and took it back. Jane followed.

The bedroom door was open and a woman stood there, smiling.
It was the woman in black!

Jane made a quick <u>curtsy</u> and Gilbert tried to bow, but it was difficult to bow with the dog in his arms!

The woman in black took the dog. 'Thank you,' she said. 'He is always trying to escape.'

Just then a soldier came round the corner.

'What do you think you are doing here?' he shouted at Jane and Gilbert, shooing them away. Then he led the woman in black back into the bedroom and slammed the door shut.

Jane and Gilbert went straight to their father and told him everything they had seen. He looked worried.

'We must tell the Master,' he said at last.

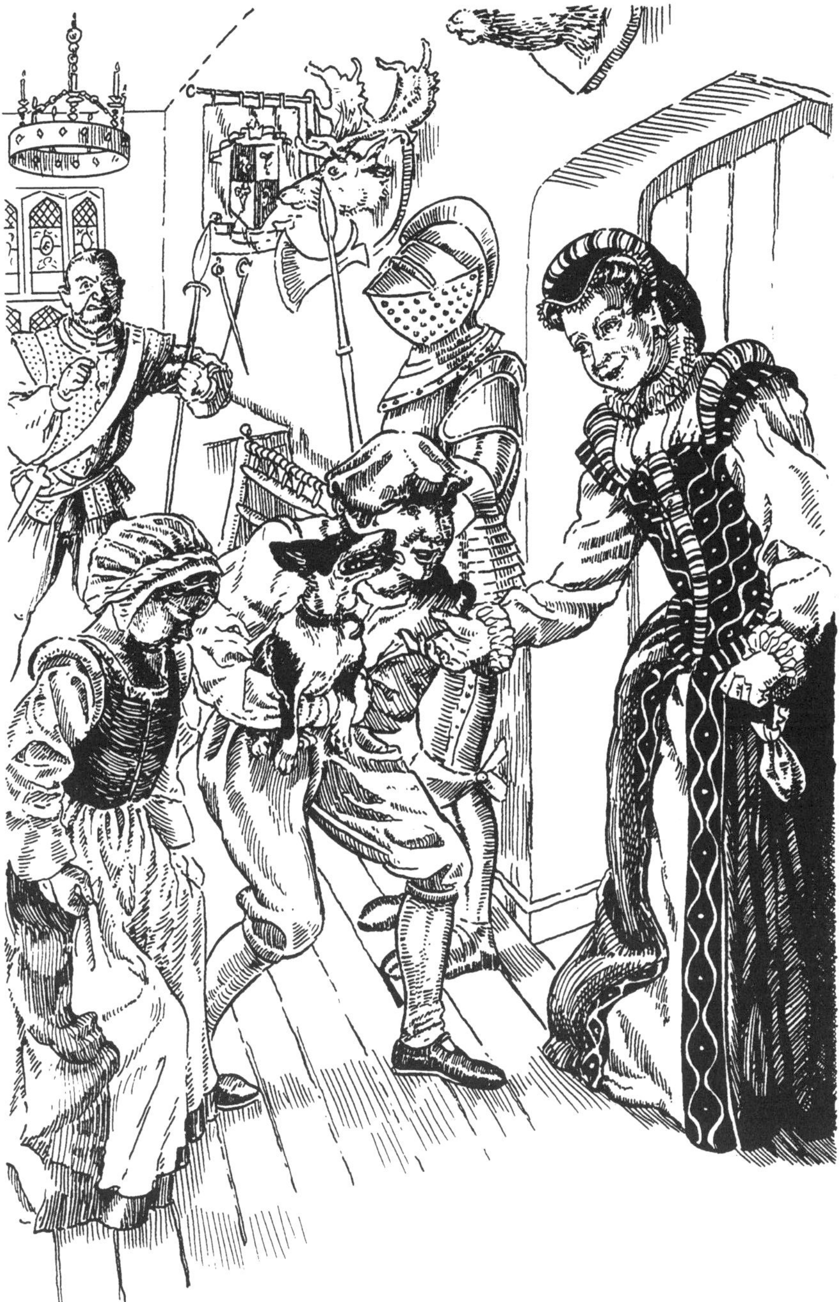

He took them along more passages to a room at the front of the house. Then he knocked and they all went inside.

Old Sir Amias, the Master, sat at a long table and listened carefully as Jane and Gilbert told him what they had seen. When they had finished, he smiled at them.

'Thank you,' he said. 'Now at last we know her secret. Now we know how she is getting messages in and out of this house.'

'Do you think there was a message in that bag?' asked Gilbert.

'I am certain of it, boy,' said Sir Amias. 'Messages come to her in the full barrels of beer and she sends replies in the empty barrels. It is a clever idea.'

'But who is she?' whispered Jane. 'Who is the woman in black. Is she a prisoner here?'

Sir Amias looked at their father. 'Can they keep another secret?' he asked. Their father nodded and Sir Amias went on.

'Yes,' he said. 'She is a prisoner here. She is a very important lady. She is Mary Stuart, the Queen of Scotland. But she is also an enemy of England and an enemy of our own Queen Elizabeth.'

'Why is that?' asked Jane, shyly.

'Mary Stuart is plotting against England,' said Sir Amias, 'and she has many friends who want to help her. But now you have discovered how she sends messages to her friends, we can find out their plans.'

Then Sir Amias stood up and gave them each a silver sixpence. 'You have done us a great service,' he said. 'I am very proud of you.'

But, as Jane left Sir Amias, she didn't feel happy. She thought of the smiling woman in black, and she felt very sad.

GLOSSARY

<u>Sir Amias</u>
Sir Amias Paulet was Mary's jailor, given the job of looking after her and making sure she did not escape

<u>cellar</u>
a great deal of beer and wine was drunk in Tudor times, and not much water. Barrels were often stored in underground rooms called cellars

<u>Chartley Manor</u>
this house, a few miles from Stafford, was once a castle. It was owned by the Earl of Essex and used for part of Mary Queen of Scots' imprisonment

<u>coach</u>
although Kings and Queens had for many years used a kind of carriage on wheels, pulled by horses, coaches for longer journeys only appeared in Tudor times. They were very uncomfortable and Queen Elizabeth preferred horseback

<u>curtsy</u>
manners in Tudor times were very important. Young boys had to learn to bow, and girls to curtsy, bending their legs, and lowering their bodies

<u>moat</u>
around castles and large houses, ditches were dug, and filled with water. These moats were for extra safety from attack, but also helped to keep prisoners in

<u>tansy</u>
a pudding made of eggs, sugar, rose water, cream and the juice of herbs, baked with butter in a shallow dish

<u>Yule log</u>
on Christmas Eve, a huge log of wood was brought into the big houses, with a special procession. The log was kept burning during Christmas. Sometimes a piece was kept to light the Yule log the next year

HISTORICAL NOTES for THE WOMAN IN BLACK

Queen Elizabeth's life was always in danger. Many plots against her were connected with King Philip of Spain, who wanted England to be a Catholic country again. This is why he sent his Armada in 1588.

Mary Queen of Scots was a Catholic, so Philip supported her. When Queen Mary was taken prisoner by the English, for plotting against Queen Elizabeth, she tried to find ways of getting secret mesages to her followers, and to Spain.

On Christmas Eve 1585 Mary was brought to Chartley Manor in Staffordshire. The house no longer exists but parts of the ruin can still be seen.

Whilst Mary was at Chartley, the strange way of sending messages by barrel was used. Letters wrapped in waterproof bags were brought in the full barrels of beer and the answers sent back in the empty barrels. Unfortunately for Mary, Elizabeth's chief spy, Sir Francis Walsingham, knew all about the letters. Queen Mary was tricked, and the letters were read.

The plot called the Babington Plot was uncovered, and Mary was moved once more, this time to Fotheringay castle in Northamptonshire. Here she was executed for treason, in February 1587.

MASTER WILL'S NEW THEATRE
1599

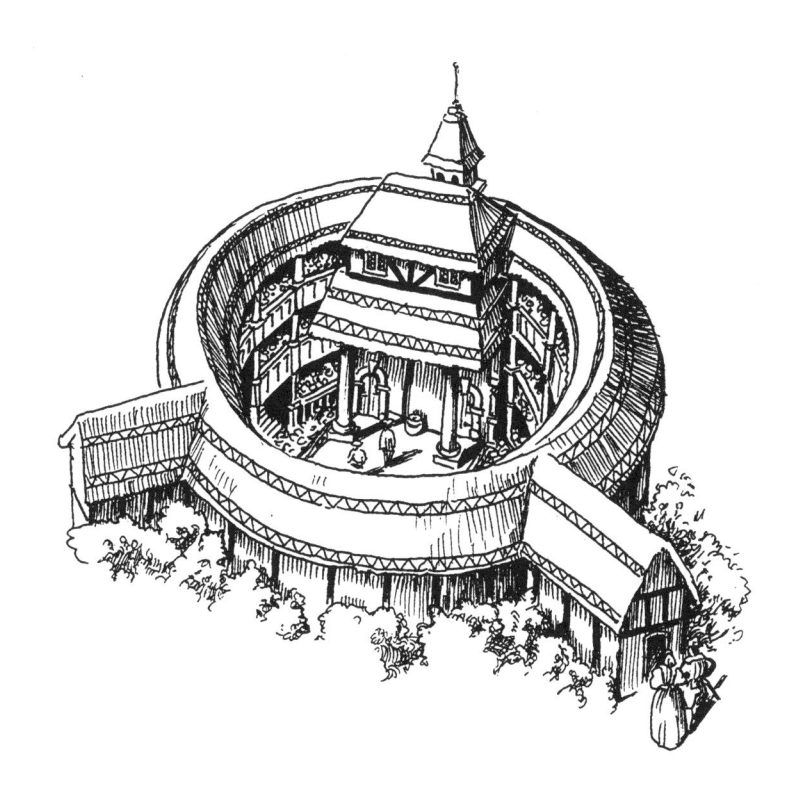

Bess opened her bedroom window and looked across Shoe Street. 'Mark,' she called.

A boy opened the top window of the house opposite.

'Can you come with me to the theatre?' asked Bess.

Mark nodded and held up a penny coin. 'I've got the money,' he said.

Bess ran down the narrow stairs to her father's shop. Her father was a shoemaker. He didn't look up from his workbench when Bess burst in.

'You're in a hurry, girl,' he said. 'What's the matter?'

'The play's on at the theatre today. Please can I have the money. Mark will come with me. You promised I could go …'

Her father smiled. 'Very well then,' he said, 'I'll give you the money if you stop dancing round like a <u>tame bear</u>.'

He gave her a penny coin and she rushed outside.

The bell of <u>Fleet Prison</u> struck one o'clock as Bess and Mark ran along Shoe Street. When they turned the corner they heard the sound of a drum and saw a small cart.

Two actors were standing on the cart. One was dressed as a <u>jester</u> and the other as a soldier. The jester was banging a drum and the soldier was shouting to the crowd:

'At the Globe Theatre, at two o'clock this very afternoon, a new play by William Shakespeare. Only one penny to see the true story of King Henry 5th.'

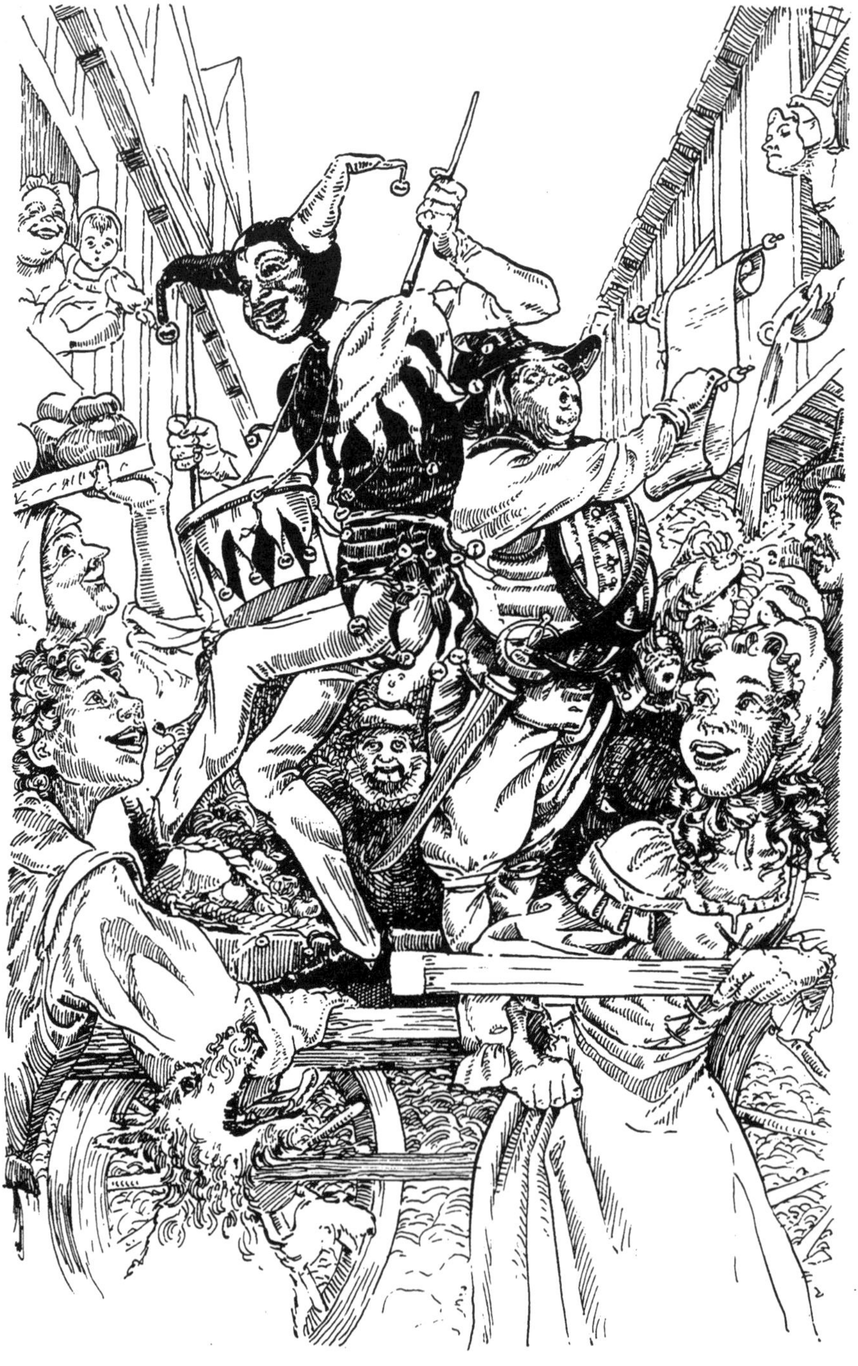

Bess and Mark had pushed through the crowd. They were standing beside the cart when the jester and the soldier jumped down from it.

'Shall we pull your cart for you?' asked Mark.

The two actors were delighted and, for the next half-hour, Bess and Mark pulled the cart through the crowded streets. Every now and then they stopped and the jester and soldier got up on the cart again and told everyone about the play.

At last they reached London Bridge, with its shops and houses. They crossed the bridge and came out into fields on the other side.

'Look, there's the Globe Theatre,' said Mark. He pointed to a tall round building with a thatched roof.

Just then a trumpet sounded from a tower on the roof of the theatre.

'That means the play will soon begin,' said the jester.

When they reached the theatre, Bess and Mark were let in free because they had pulled the cart. They went in the main door and then through a small tunnel. When they came out of the tunnel they were in the open air again.

They were in the place called the <u>pit</u> and all round the edge of the pit were rows of seats. The seats were already full and the crowd standing in the pit was large and noisy. Everyone in the pit pushed and shoved and tried to get close to the stage.

The best seats were on the stage itself. A man near Bess was laughing and pointing at the rich men sitting there smoking pipes.

A lady carrying a basketful of oranges walked past.

'Let's have an orange,' said Bess. 'We still have our money.' She bought two oranges for half a penny.

Then the curtains at the back of the stage opened and the play began. A finely-dressed actor explained that King Henry was getting ready to fight the French.

Mark and Bess were thrilled with the play. They watched every movement and listened to every word. It was very exciting.

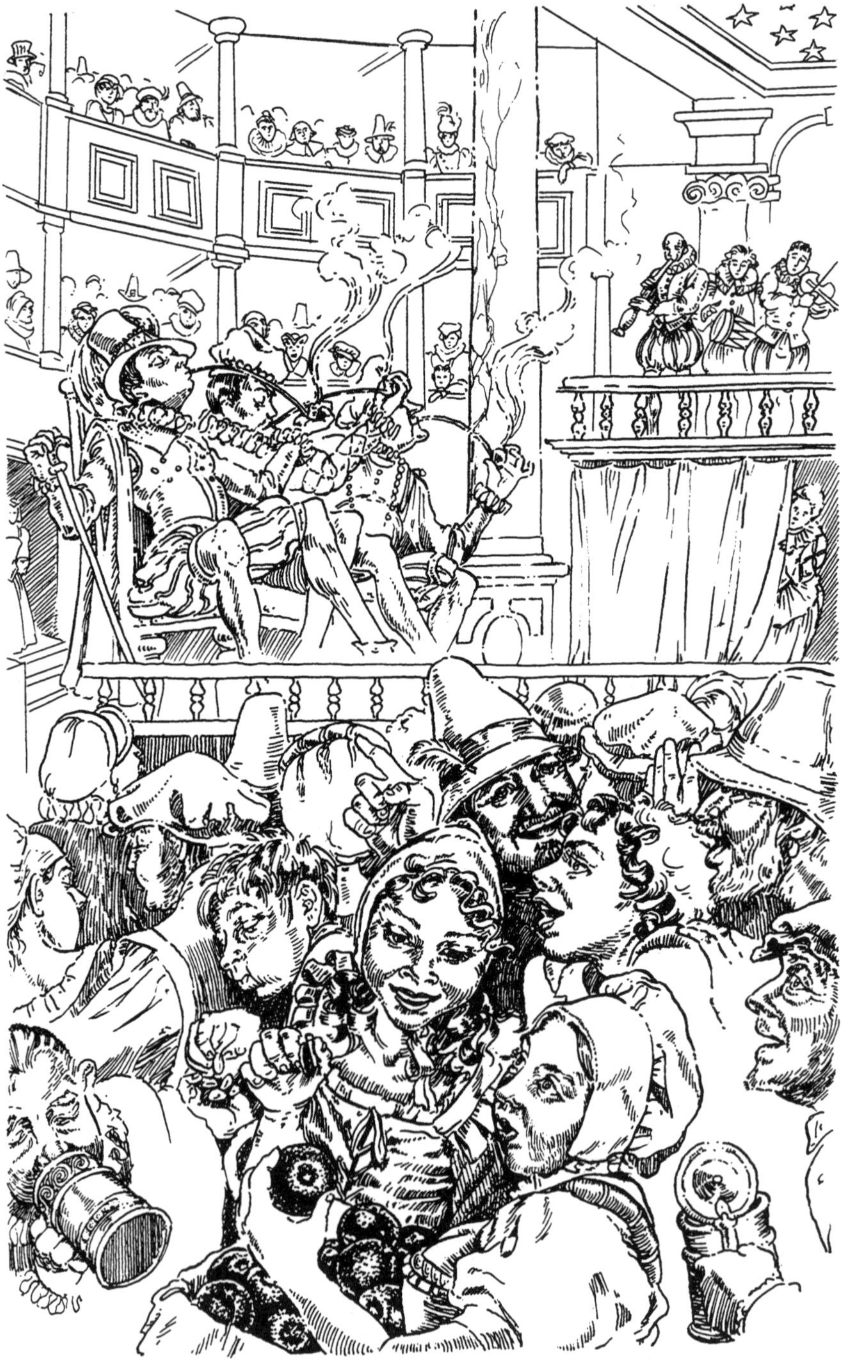

Halfway through the play there was an interval and their friend the soldier came up to them.

'Can you help us again?' he asked.

They nodded and followed him through a door into the actors' room. Everyone was getting ready for the battle scene. There were pieces of armour and weapons everywhere.

The soldier picked up two cannon-balls. 'Can you take these up to the hut?' he asked.

'How do we get there?' asked Bess.

The soldier explained that the hut was right at the top of the theatre, beside the tower. Bess and Mark carried the heavy cannon-balls up some steep stairs. In the hut at the top of the stairs there was an old man on his hands and knees.

'About time too,' he shouted. 'Put the cannon-balls in that box on the floor.' Then he got up and looked down into the theatre.

'They're ready to start the play again,' he said. He rolled the cannon-balls around in the box to make a sound like thunder.

When he'd finished, he said, 'It's the battle scene now. I have to make lots of bangs and crashes.'

Bess and Mark saw a string of fireworks hanging by the window. A long match was burning close by, ready to light them.

'Let's go,' said Mark. 'We're missing the play!'

They had just reached the top of the stairs when Bess stopped. She sniffed.

'What's that smell?' she said.
'It's only the match,' said Mark. 'Come on, hurry!'

But Bess took no notice. She ran back to the hut. The wind had blown the flame from the match onto the roof. The thatch was on fire and the old man hadn't seen it!

Bess found a long stick to beat the flames, then she dragged a stool to the window. She climbed up, but she couldn't reach the flames with the stick.

She could see down into the theatre where some of the people were pointing at the fire.

'Quick, pass me that jug of ale,' she yelled.

Mark grabbed the ale. The old man turned round.

'What do you think you are doing?' he shouted.

Bess threw the whole jugful of ale at the burning thatch. Some of the ale went over the people below. There was shouting and laughter, but there was also a loud sizzling noise, and the flames went out.

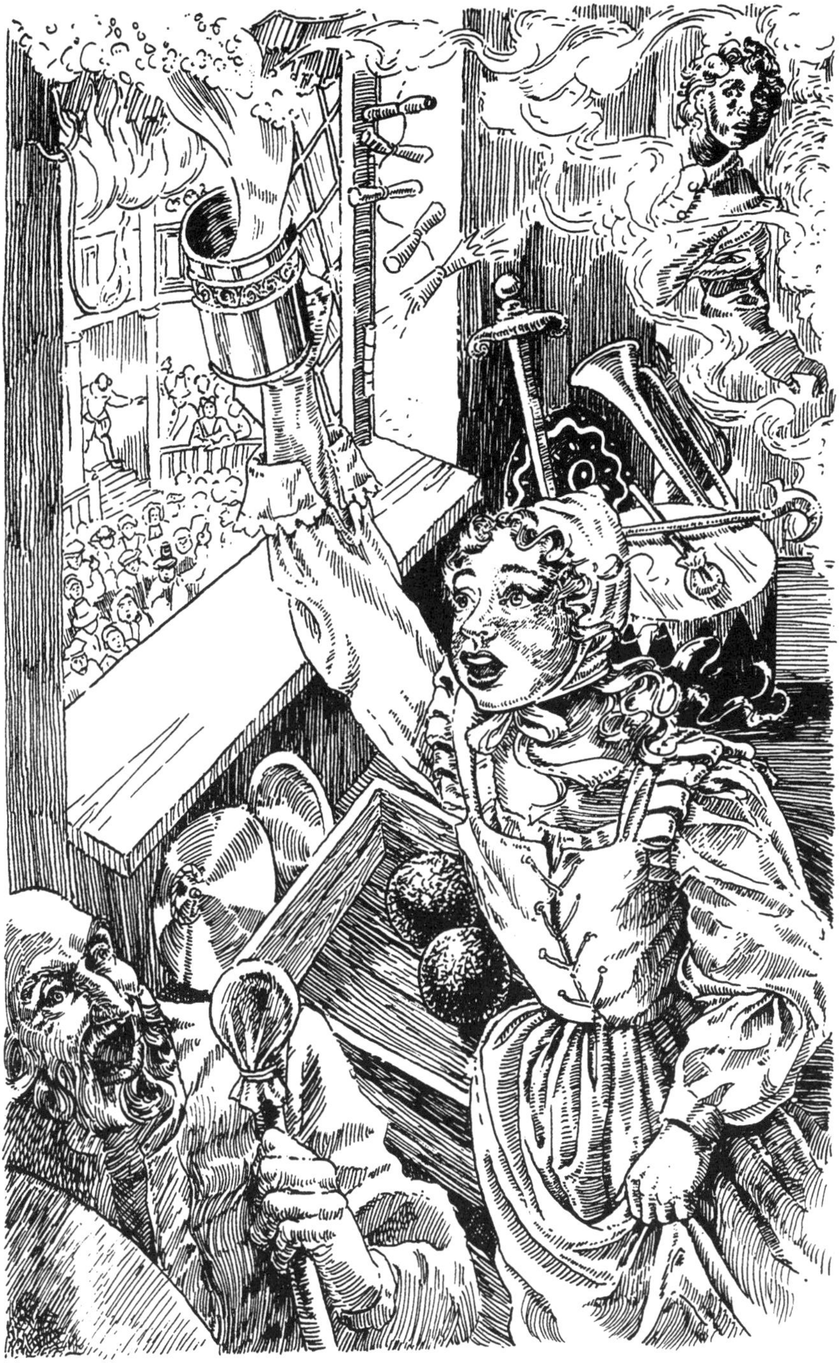

Later, the actors let Mark and Bess watch the rest of the play from the best seats. When it was over and the last cheer had died down, they saw a tall man coming towards them.

Bess nudged Mark. 'I think that's Master Shakespeare!' she whispered.

Will Shakespeare was very pleased that the play had gone so well, but he was even more pleased with Bess and Mark.

'We've only just finished building our Globe Theatre,' he said. 'You saved it from burning down, so I think you deserve a reward.'

He put his hand inside his <u>doublet</u> and took out two small pieces of paper. He handed them to Bess and Mark. Both pieces of paper were signed with his name.

'Come and see our plays whenever you wish,' he said. 'And you will not need to pay.'

Bess and Mark were thrilled. They already knew where they would be at two o'clock the next afternoon!

GLOSSARY

doublet
a Tudor jacket, often without sleeves

Fleet Prison
this prison was mainly for people who owed money. The old prison was burnt down in the Fire of London (1666)

jester
a man who 'played the fool'. He was usually dressed in a two-coloured costume

pit
the open yard in the middle of the theatre where the 'groundlings' could stand for 1d (one old penny)

Shoe Street
the street of the shoemakers. In Tudor times there were groups of shops selling the same goods. Bread Street was the Bakers' street

tame bear
bears were taken round on chains. A cruel sport was when dogs attacked the bears

HISTORICAL NOTES for MASTER WILL'S NEW THEATRE

William Shakespeare was born in Stratford upon Avon in 1564 but spent much of his life in London. He joined a group of actors, and in 1599 helped to build the Globe Theatre on the south bank of the River Thames, outside the City of London.

Theatres in Shakespeare's day were open to the weather and they needed daylight for the performances. The poorest people (the groundlings) payed one penny to stand near the stage. Richer people payed up to 12 pennies, a great deal of money in Tudor times, to sit in the galleries, or even on the edge of the stage, where they could show-off.

From a distance, the Globe looked round in shape, but was probably

20-sided. It was built of wood and plaster, with a roof of reeds. Fire was always a danger and in 1613, the first Globe was completely destroyed. The fire was started after a cannon effect went wrong! It was re-built, but this time with a tiled roof.

In London it is possible to see what the Globe Theatre was like, because an exact copy has been built very near the spot where Shakespeare's Globe stood.